T0209859

When Your Light is Gone

Jalisa Loggins

WESTBOW
P R E S S®
A DIVISION OF THOMAS NELSON
& ZONDERVAN

Copyright © 2021 Jalisa Loggins.

All rights reserved. No part of this book may be used
or reproduced by any means, graphic, electronic, or
mechanical, including photocopying, recording, taping or
by any information storage retrieval system without the
written permission of the author except in the case of brief
quotations embodied in critical articles and reviews.

WestBow Press books may be ordered through
booksellers or by contacting:

WestBow Press
A Division of Thomas Nelson & Zondervan
1663 Liberty Drive
Bloomington, IN 47403
www.westbowpress.com
844-714-3454

Because of the dynamic nature of the Internet, any web
addresses or links contained in this book may have changed
since publication and may no longer be valid. The views
expressed in this work are solely those of the author and do
not necessarily reflect the views of the publisher, and the
publisher hereby disclaims any responsibility for them.

Any people depicted in stock imagery provided by Getty Images are
models, and such images are being used for illustrative purposes only.
Certain stock imagery © Getty Images.

ISBN: 978-1-6642-4152-7 (sc)
ISBN: 978-1-6642-4151-0 (e)

Library of Congress Control Number: 2021915077

Print information available on the last page.

WestBow Press rev. date: 08/11/2021

In 2018, 25,000 cases of missing children was filed under the national center for missing and exploited children.

Every 40 seconds in the United States, a child becomes missing or abducted.

Youth Crisis Hotline
Text "Home" to 741741
For anyone: www.thehopeline.com

In Phoenix, Arizona, there was a small neighborhood where the Thompson family lived. They were Mary, David, and their son, Eric. Mary was a thirty-five year old nurse. She had straight blonde hair that went past her shoulders just an inch. She worked at Romeos' Hospital. She had been married to David for five years. David was thirty-six and had short brown hair. He was a mechanic and owned Thompson's Auto Parts. Their son, Eric, was five years old. He had short brown hair and a laugh that lit up the room.

They lived in a brown one-story house with blue shutters. Eric had his own room full of toys. He had a kid's twin bed and a dresser packed with clothes. Mary and David had their own bedroom, of course. They each had their own dressers, a queen-sized bed, and a Vizio TV. They also each had their own vehicles. Mary drove a 2018 blue Toyota Corolla. David drove a black 2018 Honda Ridgeline truck and he mainly used it for work.

An alarm went off at 6:00 a.m. David woke up and turned it off. He yawned and looked at his wife. She's beautiful, he thought. Even with messy hair. He started to wake her.

"Hey, wake up," he said as he shook her shoulders.

"No, I don't want to," she mumbled under her breath. She still had her eyes closed.

"Yes, we have to wake up Eric and go to work," he told her as he kissed her forehead. He then got out of bed, stretched, and walk to the bathroom.

While he was getting ready in the bathroom, Mary finally got out of bed. She yawned and stretched her body. She went to her closet near the bed to pick out clothes. She got out pink scrubs and gray tennis shoes. She walked over to her dresser and looked in the mirror above it. She grabbed a ponytail holder on the dresser and put it in her hair. She then walked to the bathroom and brushed her teeth. Then when Mary walked toward Eric's room, David came out of the bathroom. He was wearing a mechanic's outfit with his buisness's name on the front.

He walked in Eric's room and saw Mary getting him ready for the day. She dressed him in a red shirt, gray shorts, and black shoes.

"Hey, Daddy," he said to David. He also gave him a smile.

"Hey, buddy, are you ready to see the neighbors today?" David asked him as they walked out of the room.

"Yeah, Dad. I want to go play!" Eric exclaimed. He started running toward the kitchen. His parents walked in behind him.

In the kitchen, they had a brown table with three brown chairs. Eric sat in one while David and Mary made breakfast. They made pancakes, eggs, and bacon. Eric had a plate of pancakes and orange juice. After all three of them ate their food, Mary picked up the dishes. She put them in the sink to wash later. Then they walked to the front door. They walked out and went toward the neighbors' house. Mary and David picked up Eric by his hands and swung him. Eric laughed. That sweet laughter was their everything, their light. They put him down when they arrived at the neighbor's house. Their neighbors were Elizabeth and Peter Oswald. Elizabeth also worked as a nurse with Mary. She was thirty-five and had black curly hair. Peter worked at a plumbing factory. He was thirty-six with short black hair and was a little on the chubby side.

David knocked on the door, and the Oswalds answered. They were happy to see their friends. They regularly babysat when Mary and David worked. Eric hugged them both and said bye to his parents. He then ran into the Oswalds' living room and sat on the couch. Mary turned to Elizabeth.

"So are you sure you don't want to work for me today?" Mary asked with a smile. Elizabeth gave her an unsure look.

"Uh, no thanks," she replied. Then she laughed about it.

"Well, let's go before we're late," David said as he gently pulled on Mary's arm.

"OK, OK. Well, thanks again for watching him," Mary said.

They walked away and waved at their friends. They kissed each other and got into their own vehicles. They waved once more to each other and drove off.

Mary drove off to a white three-story building. It was an old hospital. It had been there for over twenty years, but she had only worked there for three. It was the same hospital where Eric was born. Mary remembered when she found out she was pregnant. She and David had been so excited. Throughout the pregnancy, she had morning sickness and different cravings. David's parents were already gone, but her parents were still alive. Although they lived in a different state, they threw her a great baby shower. They were also there for Eric's birth. Mary's parents' names were Racheal and Paul. They were both now retired, Mary, David, and Eric only saw them for birthdays and holidays.

She finally stopped daydreaming and got out of the car. She walked inside the building and clocked in. She started her day by passing out medicine. She was also very good at helping out others when she could. She even answered call lights and helped the nursing assistants when they were busy. She had a pretty busy day, but she often wondered what David was up too.

When David got to work, he pulled up to a gray building with a couple of windows in the front. It had a black garage door where customers' vehicles could pull up. The building had his last name on the front. He got out of his truck and went through the front door. David clocked in to work near the front door by the lobby. Throughout the day, he inspected car parts, engines, and ran diagnostic tests. The building had enough space to fit three cars inside. When David took a break, he would just take one in his office. He had a desk with a chair. He also had a laptop on his desk. On the desk, he had pictures of his wife and son. He would look at the pictures when he was stressed at work. They were so important to him Mary and David both worked for the rest of the day. They both always worked hard but in the end, they couldn't wait to get home. They both pulled up to the house about the same time. They got out of their vehicles and greeted each other with a kiss.

"Do you mind going to get Eric while I shower? Please?" Mary asked her husband while they held each other. He rolled his eyes, and they kissed once again. After they let go of each other, and David walked toward the neighbor's house while Mary went to take a shower.

David knocked on the Oswalds' door. Peter answered the door. They talked for a bit. It wasn't long until Eric came running to his dad. He gave him a big hug.

"Hey, buddy. Did you have a good day?" he asked his son.

"Yes, we colored and watched TV," Eric said.

They said their goodbyes and walked back home. They walked inside their house, and Eric ran to his room. Mary got dressed in simple black shorts and a gray shirt while David showered. She then walked into Eric's room and saw him playing with some of his stuffed animals.

"Hey, let's take a bath," Mary said as she started tickling him. He laughed. Mary picked out Toy Story pj's with Woody and Buzz on the front for him to wear. Mary gave Eric a bath. He splashed and she laughed. After she bathed and dried him off, they went to the kitchen.

David was already cooking supper. They had pork chops and mashed potatoes. They also had mac and cheese, Eric's favorite. After supper, they put Eric to bed. They both kissed him and said a quick prayer for safety. Eric finally fell asleep. Mary and David quietly left his room and went to bed.

The light was shining bright through the window in the morning. Eric opened his eyes and yawned. He got up out of his bed and stretched his body. He ran out his door and to his parents' room. Then he got up on top of the bed.

"Mommy! Daddy!" Eric crawled in between them.

"Ugh. Babe, your son wants you," David told Mary while his eyes were still closed.

"Nope. Mom is sound asleep." Mary made a fake snoring sound.

"Wake up, you guys." Eric started to shake his mom and then his dad.

"OK. It's church day." Mary yawned and stretched her body. She got up out of bed and went to the bathroom.

"Come on, buddy. Let's go get some food." David grabbed Eric and put him on the floor.

When Mary came out of the bathroom, they all went to the kitchen. They ate cereal-just milk and Fruit Loops. After breakfast, David took Eric to get dressed in his room while Mary was getting dressed. David dressed Eric in a blue-collared shirt with khaki pants and black shoes. He brushed his hair and kissed him on the cheek. Eric smiled. Meanwhile, Mary got dressed with a beige sweetheart dress and tan flats. She put her hair back in a ponytail and wore a little foundation. Then she watched Eric as David got dressed. He also put on a blue shirt and khakis. He wore his gray shoes though.

They walked out the door to the car. Mary and David took turns driving, and today David drove to the Baptist church down the street. They drove up to a small brown church building with a parking lot. They got out of the vehicle and went inside. Eric got behind his parents as they walked in. Even though he had been going there ever since he was a baby, he acted shy. His parents said everyone had wanted to hold him when he was a baby.

"Hey, how are you?" Random people would say as they shook Mary or David's hand. And of course, they noticed little Eric behind his parents. They would smile and waved at him. Eric smiled back.

Eric and his parents walked to a pew and sat down. At times, Eric wouldn't sit still. He tried to stand on the pew or sit on the floor. Mary grabbed him and told him to behave. Eric sits back on the pew between his parents.

The preacher, Nathaniel, came out of a back door and prayed with everyone. He was a tall man with blonde hair. Mid-fifties. He then dismissed the kids to their class in the back of the church. Eric walked with the other kids his age to the back. They walked to a small classroom. He immediately saw his friends Abby and Stevie.

"Hey guys." Eric said as he walked up to his friends.

"Hey Eric." Stevie gave him a hug. They were the same height. Stevie is five years old and has brown hair.

"I want a hug too." Abby told Eric. She is four years old and has blonde hair. She gave Eric a hug.

They played together in class. They colored, talked and laughed. They all had a good time listening to their teacher, Ms. Elliot. Eric thought she was a nice woman. She has long brown hair with a nice smile. She always talked about Jesus in class.

Meanwhile out front, the adults had preaching. Preacher Nathaniel talked about Jesus and God. After preaching, Mary went to get Eric from his class. They met up with David outside the church. He was talking to some people. He saw his family and went to their vehicle. They got inside and drove off. When they got home, Eric couldn't wait to go play inside. They got out of the vehicle and went inside the house.

"Lets go mommy. I wanna play in my room." Eric ran off towards his room.

"How about a nap instead?" Mary walked after Eric towards his room.

"I guess that's okay. Guess I'll fix lunch." David said sarcastically. He really didn't mind fixing them lunch. He went to the kitchen. He made ham sandwiches for everyone to hold them over until supper. He started eating his sandwich when Mary and Eric came into the room.

"He wouldn't take a nap." Mary shrugged her shoulders.

"That's okay. Here. I made sandwiches until supper." David handed them both a sandwich.

They ate their food with chips and tea. After lunch, Eric went to his room to play. Mary and David watched TV in the living room. The living room had a 55' inch TV on a TV stand. The room also had a couch, a recliner and a coffee table. Eric would run in and out of the room. He played with stuff animals. Sometimes he would stop to watch TV. He liked watching cartoons but he would rather play with his toys.

Mary and David ended up watching a movie. Later that evening, they ate hot dogs and fries. After supper, Eric started to yawn. He was put to bed where he fell asleep fast. Sometimes it took him a while to fall asleep. Meanwhile, Mary and David went to their own room. They said their good nights and kissed.

The next morning, Eric was the first one to wake up. He got out of bed and went to his parent's room. He climbed on top of their bed. They were both still sleeping. He sat in between them while he started shaking their arms.

"Mommy, daddy. Wake up." After a few tries, they woke up.

"Ugh, you're up early this morning. Mary, your child is awake." David stretched his arms and yawned.

"He's your son too." Mary didn't open her eyes yet. She stretched her arms then reached out to Eric for a hug. She pulled him close and squeezed him. Eric smiled.

David rose out of bed and wiped his eyes. He stood up and went to the bathroom to get ready for the day.

"Come on mom, I'm hungry." Eric said as he go out of Mary's gasp.

"OK, OK, lets go." She got out of bed and walked to the kitchen. Eric followed her.

Mary cooked all three of them pancakes. Eric loved his parents' cooking. He ate with his parents at the table. He eventually got syrup all over his hands. After they finished breakfast, Eric washed his hands at the kitchen sink. Then David dressed him in a green shirt with khaki pants. Meanwhile, Mary was putting her scrubs. It was a normal day for everyone. Mary and David went to work while Eric stayed at the Oswald's house. They loved their jobs but once again, Mary and David couldn't wait to get off work. After work, they both met at their house. They greeted each other with a kiss and told each other about their day. This time they both went to the neighbor's house to get their son. They knocked on the door where they were greeted by Elizabeth.

They walked inside towards the living room. The house was always so clean. The Oswald's couldn't have kids of their own so their place was always clean. The

Oswald's and the Thompson's were such good friends. They enjoyed each other's company. They become quick friends when Peter and Elizabeth moved in next door. The Thompson's had only been married for seven year while the Oswald's had been married for five.

Mary and David sat in the living room and talked to each other. Eric was more focused on watching cartoons.

"So, how was he today?" David asked as he padded his hand on Eric's head. He was sitting next to his son on a brown sofa. Mary sat on the other side of Eric.

"Very good." Peter said as he came in the room. He sat down in a brown recliner next to the sofa. His wife was sitting on the opposite side of the sofa, also in a brown recliner.

"Do you want to stay for supper?" Elizabeth asked.

"Oh, no thanks. We're tired. I think we are going to head out." Mary stood up and nudged Eric to get off the sofa.

After a long day of working, Mary and David went home with their son. As they walked towards their house, they noticed something strange. A green Ford truck was parked by their vehicles on the side of the road. As soon as they got to the front door, the truck drove off. Maybe he was lost or just trying to turn around they wandered. They walked inside and thought nothing else of the truck.

As soon as they got inside, Eric ran to his room to play. Mary and David both went to change into something more comfortable.

"Hey. When can we have a date night? Maybe one of our friends could babysit one night." David mentioned as he grabbed Mary to kiss her. She looked at him with a smile then got undressed. They both put on pj's for the night.

"Let's go out on a date tomorrow?" He grabbed Mary again and pulled her close to him.

"Sounds great." She kissed him on the lips with passion.

"Ew gross." Eric said. He was at the doorway. As soon as he said something, they let go of each other. Eric laughed and ran into the living room.

Mary went into the kitchen. She began cooking a pepperoni pizza in the oven. When it was done, she took it out with oven mittens. After it cooled off, they each got two slices of pizza and a drink. After everyone got done with their food, they watched TV. They watched some cartoon movies until Eric got sleepy. He suddenly started to yawn.

"Aw, are you sleepy?" Mary gave him a hug.

"No. I wanna stay up late." Eric said but ended up yawning again.

"Alright buddy, let's go." David picked up his restless son and took him to bed. He laid him down in bed and kissed him goodnight. Eric said goodnight while his father tucked him in. Then David walked out of the room quietly. He walked towards the bedroom where his wife was waiting on him. They kissed each other, prayed and said their good nights. Before falling asleep, they thought how truly blessed they were.

One early morning, Eric woke up and climbed out of bed. He walked over to play with his toys that was laying on the floor. He played with his dinosaur figures. Then he played with Lego blocks. He tried building something but then gave up. His mind began to wonder. He stood up and raced out of his room. He went straight to his parents' room. They was already getting ready for the day.

"Boo!" Eric said as he entered the room.

"Ah! You scared me." Mary joked around as she put her hand over her chest. She gave him a smile.

"Well, look who's up early today." David went over to Eric and gave him a nudge on the head.

"Dad. Don't do that." Eric ran over to the bed. He climbed on top and began jumping.

"Eric, don't jump on the bed please." Mary grabbed Eric and sat him down on the bed. He blew his breath.

"Hey, lets go get ready." David said as he reached out for Eric's hand. Eric grabbed his dad's hand.

David took Eric to his room. He tried to ran away from David. He grabbed his son and sat him on the bed. David picked out blue jeans and a yellow shirt with a t-Rex on the front. He also put on black tennis shoes. He got Eric dressed. Dave gave Eric a hug and kiss on the cheek. Eric smiled. His smile was so contagious.

They went to the kitchen where Mary was warming up oatmeal for breakfast. It was maple and brown sugar. Mary got bowls and silverware out of the cabinet. She then filled up the bowls with oatmeal. She put them on the table where Eric and David was sitting. David was already drinking coffee. Eric had orange juice. She sat down beside them. They ate their food while it was hot. Eric got done first and ran into the living room. After a minute, David called out to him.

"Eric? What are you doing son?" Eric had been quiet every since he went into the living room.

"Watching TV." Eric responded.

David cleared off the table while Mary checked on Eric. She slowly walked behind Eric. He was sitting on the couch watching cartoons.

"Boo!" Eric jumped as soon as Mary scared him. Mary laughed.

"Mommy! You scared me!" Eric exclaimed. Mary kissed him on the cheek.

"You tried to scare me earlier." She sat down by him and gave him a hug. He gave her a big hug. She started to tickled him and he laughed.

"Hey, where's my love at?" David walked in and sat on the couch. Eric turned towards him.

"Right here!" Eric jumped on David and gave him a hug. David padded him on the back.

"Are you ready to go next door?" He asked.

"Can't I stay with you and mommy today?" Eric asked. He frowned.

"No, afraid not buddy. But hey we don't work long today. If the weather is ok, we'll play outside after work."

"Yay!" Eric started jumping on the couch.

"Don't jump on the couch son." Mary said. She grabbed him to set him down.

Eventually, it was time for work. The Thompson family went over to their neighbors' house. They dropped off Eric and said their goodbyes. Mary and David kissed then they went their separate ways. They both left for work.

Mary pulled up to the hospital. She parked her car, turned it off and got out. She let out a sigh and wondered what kind of day it was going to be. She walked inside and clocked in for work.

13

"Hey Mary, how's it going?" Another nurse, Jennifer was walking by her as she clocked in.

"Pretty good, so far. I just got here." Mary said as her and Jennifer started walking the halls.

Jennifer, a tall blonde middle aged woman, gave report to Mary. She told her what was going on. As they were talking, Mary noticed a nursing assistant having trouble with a patient. The patient was trying to hit the nursing assistant. Mary walked over to the patient. She tried talking to them. After a minute or so, Mary walked the patient back to their room.

Meanwhile, David was at his shop hard at work. There was already cars lined up when he arrived at work. After he clocked in, he started to look up orders on the computer. Everything was electronic now. He got the first customer an oil change. Then another customer came for their tires rotated. David was busy all day long. He liked working on vehicles but he liked going home too. But it wasn't time for that just yet. It was his break time though. He went to eat a sandwich that he had packed. He sat down in the employee break room. It was a small room with white walls. After eating his sandwich, he got out his phone to text Mary.

"Hey, how's work?" David text Mary.

"Good, so far. You?" She replied.

"Busy?" He replied back.

He put up his phone and went back to work. Mary was also on break. That's why she replied. For break, she was eating a salad. After break, she went back to work. She used to work twelve hours, but now she only works eight. It was a pretty normal day for both parents. Nothing to major happened.

At the Oswalds' house, Eric was playing hide and seek with Peter. Peter was running out of breath trying to find him. He then heard Eric giggling. He was in the bathroom.

"Caught ya!" Peter opened the door in a flash and Eric jumped. Peter laughed.

"Hey! That's not funny." Eric put his hand over his chest.

"What are you boys up too?" Elizabeth walked around Peter with her hands on her hips.

"He scared me!" Eric exclaimed as he pointed to Peter.

"Alright, well, how about some lunch?" Elizabeth walked towards the kitchen to fix their lunch.

"Alright bud, lets go watch tv." Peter said while him and Eric went to watch TV on the couch.

Elizabeth cooked tomato soup and grilled cheese. She brought them in the living room on plates. They ate their food with sweet tea to drink. After they ate, they watched Looney Tunes. Eric sometimes would color in a coloring book. Eventually he took a nap on the couch. When he woke up, he noticed his parents was in the same room.

"Hey bud, are you ready to go home?" David said as he sat next to Eric.

"Yeah." Eric said with a yawn.

Eric and his parents left the neighbors' house. When they got near the house, a green truck was pulling out of their driveway. The truck pulled forward, backed out and left.

"Hey, wasn't that the same green truck from the other day?" Mary asked David as they walked closer to their house.

David shrugged his shoulders. They went inside to change clothes. Mary changed into black shorts and a gray shirt. David had blue shorts on with a white shirt.

They met up in the living room where Eric was sitting on the couch.

"Hey, lets go outside to play." Eric said as he got a blue ball to play with.

They all went outside to play catch. They laughed and had a good afternoon. When it started to get dark, they went inside. They had pork chops and mashed potatoes that David cooked. After a while, Eric started to yawn. David picked him up and carried him to bed. Meanwhile, Mary washed the dishes and cleaned the kitchen. After she got done, she met up with David in their bedroom. They kissed and got in bed. After kissing for a while, they fell asleep pretty fast.

"Mommy! Daddy!" Eric yelled waking David and Mary.

"Eric, what's wrong?" Mary said as she yawned.

"Why are you not in your bed son?" David asked as he sat up in the bed.

"I had a nightmare. It was scary." Eric climbed in between his parents.

"It was just a dream. It wasn't real." Mary rubbed Eric's back.

"Something bad is going to happen." Eric said as he leaned on his mom.

"No, its not. Everything is okay. Just sleep with us tonight." David laid back in the bed.

"Okay." Eric laid in the middle of his parents and finally fell asleep.

$\mathcal{E}$ ric opened his eyes and yawned. He shielded his eyes from the bright sunshine from the window. He climbed out of his parents' bed. They wasn't in the room so he went into the kitchen. They was getting breakfast ready for the morning.

"Look who's awake." David said as he was getting a cup of coffee.

David started drinking his coffee while Mary cooked breakfast. Eric walked towards the table and sat down in a chair.

"Guess what? We're off work today." Mary said. She cooked them all bowls of oatmeal.

"Yay!" Eric said. Mary put oatmeal on the table. Eric drank orange juice while Mary drank coffee.

"Can we play outside today?" Eric asked.

"I guess we can." David said with a smile.

"Good, because I want to play catch." Eric said. He also was smiling.

They ate their food and cleaned up the kitchen.

"Lets go put on some play clothes." Mary said as her and Eric went to his room.

Mary picked out gray shorts and a blue shirt for Eric to wear. After changing clothes, he quickly grab a rainbow color ball.

"Hey, wait a second, you have to put on your shoes." Mary said as she grab a pair of black tennis shoes.

She put on the shoes on Eric. Then he ran into the living room with his ball. He loved playing outside. So, he was very excited about playing catch with his parents. They finally went outside. They tossed the ball around. Then, Mary decided to fix them some drinks.

"Hey boys, I'll be back. I'm going to fix us some drinks." Mary said as she walked inside. Then she began calling them inside to get a drink.

"Come on inside son." David called for his son as he began walking inside. Eric was right behind him until he accidentally dropped his ball. It started rolling down the driveway while a green truck started to slowly pull up.

The truck stopped in front of the driveway. A tall older bald man got out of the truck. He picked up the ball that rolled in front of him. Eric looked at the man. All the man could see was a lost boy.

"Hey, here you go son." The bald man said as he gave the ball back.

And just like that, the man grabbed Eric.

"Hey let go!" Eric yelled. The man put Eric in his truck.

Meanwhile, David and Mary was yelling for Eric to come inside. When they both walked outside, it was too late. They saw a green truck drive off with their son.

"Eric!" Mary yelled.

"No! Stop!" David yelled. They both ran out into the road.

David got out his phone and called the police. Mary started breathing hard.

"Yes, hello? My son was just kidnapped!" David told the police. Mary started pacing around. She started to cry. David hung up the phone after giving the police their address.

"Honey, the police are on their way." David said as he hugged his wife.

After walking inside, they hugged each other again. They were both upset. They couldn't believe something like this happened. They let go of each other when they heard police sirens. They met the police outside their driveway. A tall skinny cop with brown hair got out of a cop car.

"Hey, I'm Officer Johnson. Someone called about a kidnapping?" He said as he walked up towards the Thompsons.

"Yes, a green Ford truck took our son. Please help us." Mary responded.

"Did you see who was in the truck?" The officer asked with hands on his hips.

"No, we didn't." David said.

They both told the officer what had happened. Their breakfast, playing outside and after. They thought Eric was right behind them.

"OK, let me send in a report and I will get back to you as soon as I can." Officer Johnson said. Then he got into his car and left.

Mary and David both held each other as they sat on their couch. They cried into each other's arms until David looked at Mary.

"Hey, I'm going to get Peter next door to go look for Eric, okay?" David said. He stood up from up from the couch and grabbed his keys.

"Wait, I need to go too." Mary said.

"No, just stay here. Don't worry, we will find him. said. He leaned over and kissed Mary on the lips.

David ran over to the Oswalds and explained what happened. Peter and Elizabeth was in shock. After explaining everything, Elizabeth went over to see how Mary was doing. Meanwhile, David and Peter went to look for Eric. Peter drove his 2018 black Honda Accord. While Elizabeth was consoling Mary, Peter tried not to speed but he knew Eric's life could be in danger. They tried looking for the green truck that took Eric.

Meanwhile, after the bald man kidnapped Eric, he took him to his house. Eric had been crying all the way there. The man actually tried to calm Eric down but it didn't work. The bald man told Eric that he was going to babysit Eric for a while. He then took Eric inside of his house. It was a small house. When they walked inside, they walked into the living room.

"What are we doing here?" Eric asked.

"This is my house. Your room is in there." The bald man answered and pointed to a nearby room.

Eric walked in the room. He saw a small bed with toys. A dresser that held clothes in them. Eric turned around to face the man.

"I want to go home." Eric said.

"You are home. Play with some toys while I fixed dinner." He replied. He then went into the kitchen.

Eric, still scared, found toys to play with. They had calmed him down in a way. He continued to play with legos and blocks. Then the bald man came into the room.

"Come on, lets eat." He said. Eric was hungry so he followed behind him. He had made tomato soup and grilled cheese sandwiches. Eric ate until he was full.

"Where is my mommy? I want my mom!" Eric exclaimed as he looked at the bald man.

"Well, she's not here. Lets go to bed, okay? Tomorrow will be a better day." The bald man said.

Eric looked like he was going to cry again. So, the bald man picked him up and started tickling him. Eric laughed as they went back to the kid's room. Eric thought the man was nice and that he might just watch him for a little while. Maybe his mommy and daddy was at work. The bald man put Eric in the bed and covered him up with blankets.

"I hope you stay little forever. Goodnight." He told Eric. He then left the room and went to his own bedroom to sleep.

Eventually, Eric got sleepy. He yawned and tried to fight it. Then, he closed his eyes and fell asleep.

Mary and David woke up the next morning. They didn't sleep well the night before. They both thought it was all a dream. Both of them was checking their phone for any news. No news yet. They was just receiving texts and posts saying people was praying for them. They looked at each other with sadness. Then, they hugged each other. They cuddled for what seemed like a while. They had both taken off for the day. Mary got out of bed and went to the kitchen. David followed her. They drank coffee and ate a quick bite of toast. Neither of them had an appetite. After they finished, they each started calling people on their contact list. Still nothing.

"I don't know what to do anymore. We need help." Mary finally spoke up.

"We need to pray. Maybe, we could go talk to the preacher." David said.

"Maybe later. Can we just ride around please?" Mary asked.

"Okay, lets go." David said. He wanted to tell her that him and Peter drove around a lot last night. He didn't want to upset her though.

They both got in David's truck and drove around. They were looking for something. Anything. Mary called the police to see if they had any news. Nothing yet. She looked even more upset after the call. David kept driving around the city. They couldn't find any sign of the truck. They eventually drove back home. When they got out of David's truck, the Oswalds' walked over to them. Elizabeth and Peter sat on their couch the Thompson's living room.

"Have you heard anything yet?" Elizabeth asked.

"No, not yet." Mary responded.

There was an awkward pause. Mary and David also took a seat in the living room. Suddenly, Mary's phone rang. She thought it was the police, but it was her mom.

"Hello?" Mary answered.

"No, mom, we haven't found anything out yet. Just stay at home with dad okay?" Mary said on the phone.

"Okay. I love you too." Mary told her mom. When she hung up the phone, David was looking at her.

"Well? Did she want to come over?" David asked.

"Yeah, but I told her to come. They can come up whenever Eric comes home." Mary responded.

Elizabeth and Peter both looked at each other. What if Eric never came home? They tried not to think that way. They didn't want to upset Mary or David. They already looked scared.

Elizabeth offered to cook them food. They both refused but eventually gave in. Elizabeth and Peter walked back to their house to start cooking. They both cooked pork chops and mashed potatoes. After they finished cooking, they brought it over to their neighbors' house. They also brought over sweet tea. They said grace before they ate. Nobody said much that night. Elizabeth was kind of to clean up their dishes. Eventually, they left and went home. Mary and David was both drained. They went to bed. Mostly that night, Mary cried that night. She often wondered what Eric did day.

Earlier that day, Eric once again asked the bald man when he was going home.

"I told you that you are home." He said.

Eric looked sad. The bald man picked up toys from the kid's room. He encourage Eric to play with him. Eric picked up some blocks and started building a tower. The bald man and Eric played all day. After they played, they ate chicken fingers for supper. After supper, Eric took a bath. The bald man made sure that Eric washed himself off. When Eric got out of the bath, the bald man gave him new clothes to wear. Eric wore a gray shirt and black shorts to bed. They fit him just perfectly.

"When can I see my mom?" Eric asked as the bald man was laying him down in the bed.

"She's gone. But you know what? I'm here. We can play everyday and eat whatever you want." He said.

"I guess so." Eric yawned and went to sleep soon after.

"I love you." The bald man said. He touched his forehead and brushed his hair back. He then went to his own room and went to sleep.

As a couple of days went by, the Thompson family still hadn't received any news on Eric. David and Mary finally decided to go back to work. They were still feeling depressed but they had bills to pay. They didn't want them to start pilling up. Before they left for work, they kissed each other goodbye on the cheek. They muttered under their breath a "I love you" and a "goodbye". They got into their vehicles and left for work. Neither of them wanted to listen to the radio so they drove in silence. Mary finally arrived at work. After clocking in, she felt like everyone was looking at her. People was randomly look at her and ask how she was. She felt terrible but didn't want anyone to know. She did her rounds and passed out medicine to her patients.

She would often pass by CNAs. The patients seem like they was giving them a hard time. Mary just passed by and didn't say a word. She even had a thought, "Why should I help them if God isn't going to help me?" She felt like a zombie for the rest of the day. He tried to keep busy but it didn't help. Nothing helped. He kept getting aggravated if someone asked him if he was okay.

Although, he said he was fine, on the inside he was heartbroken. He didn't want to show it at work.

After both having long days at work, they finally came back home and would call Officer Johnson. They called him every afternoon. They would always end up depressed or crying after each call. The police didn't even have a lead yet.

One afternoon, David and Mary decided to talk to preacher Nathaniel. They wanted his advice. They were beginning to feel like God had left them. They needed help. They both rode to the church in Mary's car. When they arrived to the church, they both let out a sigh. They got out of the car and went inside. It was raining so they practically ran inside. Mary regretted wearing blue jeans and a pink sweater to church. She usually wears dresses or shirts. As they went inside, she looked at David. He looked so handsome, she thought. She didn't know why she didn't tell him. He was wearing a gray button up shirt and blue jeans.

After getting inside the church, they sat down on a pew. Preacher Nathaniel came from one of the back doors of the church. He walked towards them and David stood up to shake his hand. The preacher was a tall man with blonde hair. He was most likely in his forties.

"Thanks for meeting with us today." David said as he sat back down on the pew. The preacher then shook Mary's hand. He then sat down on the pew in front of them but turned so he could see them while they talked.

"Have you heard anything yet?" He asked.

"No, not yet. We don't know what to do anymore. We need your advice." Mary said. She tried not to cry. Mary looked down as David held her hand.

"My prayers isn't working." Mary continued to say. She looked up at the preacher with tears in her eyes.

"Why do you think your prayers isn't working? Because your son isn't back? That doesn't' mean God isn't listening." He said with a concerned face.

"Well, God isn't' listening to any of our prayers." Mary said as she glanced over at David. She was upset. She just wanted her son back. She knew David felt the same way.

"Don't lose faith over this. God is always listening." Preacher Nathaniel said.

"We just don't feel like he's there." David said. He squeezed Mary's hand.

"Although we don't know the plans that God has, we must trust him. He's big enough to handle our issues. It may not seem like things are good but God is always working to bring a good outcome." The preacher said.

There was a pause, a moment of silence. They all looked at each other. Then the preacher continued to talk.

"Do you understand that God wants the best for you? If you have faith in God, then why not turn your life to him? Trust in him." He said.

"I don't think we're ready to give up hope. We know God is in control but' David looks at his wife then continues, 'we just want our son back." David said. The preacher then said a prayer over them.

Meanwhile, Eric was watching tv with the bald man. They were both sitting on the couch. They both had clothes on from the night before. Eric wanted to change earlier but the bald man said there was no need.

"Can I go see Elizabeth today?" Eric asked.

"Who's that?" The bald man asked.

"My neighbor." Eric replied.

"No, not today." He told Eric.

As a couple of more days passed, Eric asked less

questions about his parents. The bald man tried his best to distract him. It wasn't easy. Eric would play with the toys in the kid's bedroom. He continued to wear clothes in the closet that seem to fit him perfectly. The bald man had planned ahead by getting a few week's worth of food. He didn't want to leave the kid behind. Eventually, they would need more food. He knew he would have to go to the store soon. After eating supper one night, he decided to have a talk with Eric. They were sitting at a table in the kitchen eating pork chops. The bald man stopped eating and looked at Eric.

"Hey buddy. I need to talk to you about something." He said. Eric stopped eating and looked at him.

"So, I need to go to the store tomorrow and you need to stay here." He told Eric.

"Why can't I go with you? I wanna get out of this house." Eric said looking sad.

"No. You can't. You have to stay here." He said.

"But why?" Eric asked.

"Because I want you here, okay? I don't want you to distract me. Now, eat your food." He said. He started eating the rest of his food.

Eric pouted for a minute then began to eat the rest of his food also. After supper, the bald man cleaned the dishes while Eric took a bath. After he was done, he wore green pj's. He went into the kid's bedroom and climbed into bed. The bald man came into the room and tucked him in.

He explained again to Eric about going to the store alone. Finally, Eric said he understood. The bald man kissed him on the forehead and went to his own room. Eric laid in bed as he thought about his parents. He wondered when he was going to see them again. He then fell asleep.

Meanwhile, Eric's parents prayed that night. They prayed to find him but most importantly, they prayed for his safety. They didn't know what kind of person had him. They could only get the police to send out AMBER alerts and pray. And they prayed hard.

Mary and David woke up the next morning with a bright sunshine coming through the window. While they got ready for work, the bald man woke up Eric. Eric started yawning. The bald man told him to go eat breakfast. He had made Eric scrambled eggs and bacon. Eric got up from the bed and went to the kitchen. He was still yawning. The bald man fixed Eric a plate of food and gave him orange juice. Eric took his food to the living room to eat. The bald man explained to Eric again that he needed to go to the store. He turned on cartoons for Eric to watch.

"But why can't I go with you?" Eric asked.

"Because its our secret that you're here." He replied.

"Doesn't my parents know where I'm at?" Eric asked.

"Of course they do. I want you to watch tv and play with your toys while I go to the store." He said.

Eric nodded while eating. The bald man walked out the door, locked it and walked towards the truck. Eric thought he was nice. He did think about going home but he didn't know which way it was. He also thought if he tried going home, the bald man would be mad. So, he just sat, ate his food and watched TV.

After Mary got dressed for work, she went to Eric's room. She thought about him playing with his toys. She thought about tucking him into bed. Then she bent down to pick up some toys on the floor. David then walked into the room.

"Hey, there's no use in cleaning his room. He will just mess it up again when gets home." David said. He let out a tiny smile at the thought of his son playing.

"I know. I just want everything to be perfect when he gets here." Mary said.

She continued to clean his room. When she was

done, she realized it was time for work. David had made her a grilled cheese sandwich while she was cleaning. She grabbed the sandwich and they said their goodbyes. Mary ate her sandwich on the way to work. She had lost track of time this morning. Her or David wasn't late though. Talking to the preacher and praying really put them both in a better mood. They both had hope they would see their son again. They choose to not the devil ruin their day.

While they were both at work, Eric waited inside the house. After he ate, he watched cartoons and played with toys. It was just thirty minutes that that bald man had been to the store. He came through the front door with bags of groceries. He went to the kitchen to put them up in the cabinets. He then found Eric playing with toys in the kid's room.

"Hey, what are you doing son?" The bald man asked.

"Just playing. Wanna play with me?" Eric asked.

He got on the floor and they both played with legos. They build houses and other things out of blocks. They had fun. Eric enjoyed playing with legos.

A couple of days had passed by. The bald man and Eric did the same routine. They ate, played, watched tv and slept. Meanwhile, Mary and David still went to work. They kept praying hard. Their church, family and friends prayed along with them. They did go to church a couple of times. They thought at first that people would only feel sorry for them. That feeling went away when they went to church more. They would still get negative thoughts and doubts. Bad thoughts that they would never get to see their son. They just prayed and thought about their happy son. The police had kept an AMBER alert going. One day, David received a call from the police. David put his phone up to his ear.

"Hello?" David answered.

"Yes, this is Officer Johnson. We have someone that has seen the description of the vehicle that may have took your son." He told David.

"What? That's wonderful news!" David exclaimed.

"What is it? Whats going on?" Mary asked as she looked at David. David held up his hand.

"The witness said they saw the vehicle at the local store twenty miles away. They didn't get a good look at the driver, just the truck." The officer explained.

He also said he would keep them updated. When David got off the phone, he told Mary what happened. Mary was sitting down at the time but when David told her, she jumped up and hugged him. She cried tears of joy. With the AMBER alert, they can also put out an alert for the vehicle. They both hugged and kissed each other. They was thrilled.

After a few hours had passed, the AMBER alert had updated. Now, the alert included the description of the vehicle that took Eric. Family and friends started calling the Thompsons. They asked everyone that called to keep Eric in their prayers. They also asked them to keep a look out on a 2015 green Ford truck. After several phone calls, they prayed for their son. Mostly for him to be found.

A few more days had passed. One day, the bald man cooked Eric pancakes and turned on the tv. The bald man had to go to the store again. Before he left, he told Eric to stay in the house. Eric nodded. While the bald man was out, Eric ate his breakfast. He watched tv and also played with toys.

His parents on the other hand was both off for the day. They just wanted to relax but soon, the negative thoughts began to enter their minds.

"What if whoever has Eric does bad things to him?" Mary though while sitting on the couch. She glanced at David, who was sitting next to her. Then she went back to watching TV. She also grabbed a pillow and held it.

"She looks comfortable in her pink pjs. But I know shes worried. What if Eric never comes home?" David thought. He was wearing pjs also. Well, his version of pjs. It was just a white shirt and black shorts. He grab Mary and pulled her close to him. He held her in his arms as they both watched TV.

Meanwhile, the bald man finally arrived at the local store. He parked right in front of the store. He got out of his truck and went inside. He stuffed his keys in his jacket pocket. Besides the jacket, he had on blue jeans and a gray shirt. Once inside, he gathered some items for his house. After checking out, he over heard a clerk talking to a manager. The clerk recognized the truck that he got out of. The bald man hurried out of the store after checking out. He was off the parking lot before the police was called.

When he arrived back at his house, he rushed in the front door. It scared Eric at little. Eric was sitting on the couch. The bald man came through and went to the kitchen. He went to put up the groceries then he came back into the living.

"What is happening?" Eric asked.

"Nothing. Just too many people at the store." He said. He looked out of breath as he sat next to Eric on the couch.

"I guess I will try another store next time." He said. Eric just looked at him in wonder.

They continued to watch TV. Eventually, they ate chicken fingers and fries. Then Eric took a bath. When he came out fully dressed, he saw the bald man crying.

31

He was sitting on his bed looking at pictures. Once he noticed Eric, he put away the pictures in a drawer.

"Can I not see the pictures?" Eric asked. His hair was still wet from the shower.

"No. They are too special to me." He said. He looked at Eric and smiled.

"But you are also special to me." He picked up Eric and took him to the other room. He laid him in bed and said his good nights. Then he went back to his room and fell asleep.

The next morning came with a bright ray of sunshine. Officer Johnson called Mary on her cell phone. It was still morning so Mary and David was still in bed. Mary woke up to her phone ringing. She raised up, yawned and answered her phone. David also woke up.

"Hello?" Mary answered.

"Who is it?" David looked at Mary and asked. She ignored him though.

"That sounds great! Thank you for letting me know!" Mary exclaimed. She hung up the phone and started smiling.

"What? Did something happen?" David asked. He sat straight up in the bed.

"Officer Johnson said the clerk from the local store called again. The clerk got a look at the man who kidnapped Eric. The police are updating the AMBER alert and putting in his description. Isn't that great news?" She was smiling really big.

"Yes! That's great news." David got excited. He was smiling but then he got a concerned look on his face.

"It seems like getting closer but it still feels like hes far away." He said. Mary kissed him on the lips.

"We're going to find him. Don't worry." She said.

The next few days was the same for Eric and the bald man. They just kept doing what they continued to do. They ate, played together, watch tv and slept. Today though, Eric could tell it was sunny outside through the windows.

"Can I go play outside?" Eric asked.

"No, its too hot outside." The bald man responded.

"I'll wear shorts. Please?" Eric started to whine.

"I said no." He responded angrily.

Eric felt restricted. He couldn't see his parents or play outside. He got upset and ran to the kid's room to play. The bald man looked sad as well, but he didn't want anything to happen to Eric.

The same has been going on for the Thompsons too. They work, eat, sleep and pray for Eric's returned. They also worried about his safety. It was just a cat and mouse game but they were sitting ducks. They wanted to do something but what could they do?

Meanwhile, the bald man went to talk to Eric.

"Hey bud, why don't we play outside after I go to the store tomorrow?" He asked.

"Really? Yeah please." Eric got excited. He was so excited that he could barely sleep that night. He loved playing outside. Any kid does.

The next morning, he woke up and got out of bed. He was in the kitchen already making pancakes.

"When can we go outside?" Eric asked as he sat in a dining room chair.

"After I come back from the store. Be patient son." He said. He paused dead in his tracks. His face went blank. He just stared into space.

"You ok?" Eric asked. He came back to reality.

"Yeah. I'm fine." He said. He got Eric a plate of pancakes and orange juice.

They both ate in the kitchen. After they were done, they left the dishes in the sink. Eric ran to the kid's room. He found blue jeans and a blue shirt to wear. After he changed clothes, he put on his own shoes to wear. The bald man came into the room.

"Hey, I'm going to the store now. You have to stay here, okay? Play with your toys while I'm gone." He said.

He left the room and left for the store. Eric stayed in the kid's room. He played with legos and other toys. Then eventually, he got bored and went to watch tv.

When the bald man left for the store, he had to chose a different one. He didn't want to be spotted. He got out of his truck and walked inside. It was just a different store from the other side of town. He felt like he was being watched as soon as he entered the store. He went down some aisles and noticed a cop walking towards way. He tried to walk away but it was to late. It was a blur of what happened next. The officer arrested him. He couldn't remember everything but he remember him reading his rights. He then put him into a police car, After they arrived at the police station, he got his fingerprints and picture taken. Then he got put in a cell. He was nervous and scared. The same officer that booked him starting asking question.

"Sir, I am officer Johnson. I need to ask you some questions. You didn't respond to them at the store. What is your name?" He asked. He was standing outside of the cell.

"Arthur Mathews." He responded. He was shaking and still nervous.

"Please sir, I have to get back to my son." He said.

"Your son? Where is Eric Thompson, Arthur?" He asked as he was getting closer to the bars of the cell. His voice was calm, but he wanted to get angry with him.

"My son, wait, he's... I don't know where Eric is." Arthur responded. He was shaking his head. He was confused.

"Where is Eric?" Officer Johnson asked.

"I don't know who that is." Arthur said. He was scared.

Officer Johnson turned around and left Arthur in the cell. He went to his desk and called the Thompson family.

Mary and David was sitting on the couch. They were going to watch a movie when the Mary's phone rang. She answered her phone.

"Hello?" Mary answered. David and her both looked at each other.

"Hey, Ms. Thompson. This is officer Johnson. I just wanted to update you. We have the kidnapper that took Eric in questioning." He said. Mary gasped.

"What? Have you found Eric? What happened to my son?" She kept asking. She was beginning to look worried.

"What? What's wrong, honey?" David asked as he put a hand on her shoulder. Mary ignored him.

"We haven't found Eric yet. I'll call you when we find out more information." He continued. Mary ended the call and turned to David.

"They haven't found Eric but they have arrested his kidnapper." Mary said. She still looked worried.

"That's great that they have arrested him." David said. He smiled then gave Mary a concerned look.

"What's wrong?" David asked.

"Eric is out there all alone. What if someone else was involved? Where is he, David?" Mary asked. David hugged her.

"We'll find him. Don't worry." David told her as he held her in his arms.

"We need to call a lawyer." David told Mary. She looked confused.

"Why?" Mary asked.

"So, we can file charges against the kidnapper." David responded.

"I just want our son back and forget this ever happened." She said. David laid his hands on her shoulders.

"We'll get him back. But this person has to pay for what he did." He said. Once again, he hugged Mary.

"Come on. Lets go to bed and I'll call a lawyer tomorrow." He said. They went to bed and fell asleep.

When the next morning came, Arthur was greeted by a man in a suit. He had blonde shaggy hair and a briefcase.

"Hi, I'm Michael Robertson. I'm going to be your lawyer." He said with a smile.

"But I don't have the money for a lawyer." Arthur responded as he walked closer to the man.

"You only pay me if we win." He said with a laugh.

Arthur look at him strangely. Michael got out a pen and notepad out of his briefcase. Although he looked to be in his thirties, he had a hard time standing back up.

"What's wrong with you?" Arthur asked.

"Oh, I have a bad back." He said as he wrote on his notepad.

"But you're so young. You shouldn't be hurting like that." Arthur said. He was holding on the bars of the cell now.

"Yeah, okay. You tell that to kids at a hospital who is in a worse shape then we are. Age doesn't count when it comes to pain." He said.

Arthur's head must have been hurting because he grabbed his forehead in pain.

"I have a headache. Do you know where I am? I forgot." Arthur asked. He genuinely looked confused. Michael looked at him for a moment. He studied him.

"How long as it been since you went to the doctor?" Michael asked.

"It has been a while." Arthur replied. He was still rubbing his head.

"Alright, I'll see if I can get a doctor to check you out." Michael said. Arthur looked at him.

After they talked, Michael left the station. Arthur felt alone. He laid on a rusty bed and eventually fell asleep.

The next morning, the Thompsons met with a lawyer. It was at a small brown building but it had several offices inside. They walked inside and met with Henry Haddock. He looked a little overweight with brown hair. He looked to be about forty or forty-five. Somewhere in his forties. He sat at a black desk with a laptop. He was sitting in a black computer chair. He graduated from Harvard or at least that's what the frame on the wall said. It was hanging on the wall along with other pictures.

Both Mary and David talked about the kidnapping. They talked about their son and how they felt. The big time lawyer said it was cost them $50,000. Mary and David's jaw dropped.

"We can't afford that." Mary said with a hand over her chest. She looked at David.

"No, sorry. We'll just have to go somewhere else." He said. They started to stand up but Henry stopped them.

"Alright, alright. No fee unless we win. But hey, I never lose." He said with a wink.

They agreed to his terms. In all honestly, they just wanted their son back. On the way home, they wanted to talk to each other but didn't know what to say. When they finally got home, they both went to do their own separate things. Mary started on supper while David took a shower. Then he washed clothes. The eventually sat down to eat supper together. Mary finally looked at David.

"Did we do the right thing by hiring him?" She asked.

"I think so." David said. They eventually cleaned the kitchen and went to bed.

"Hey, I haven't been trying to ignore you. I just don't know what to say." David said. He pulled Mary close to him under the sheets. He hugged her tight.

"I know." Mary responded with a kiss.

They ended up holding each other for a while and fell asleep.

A couple of days later, the Thompsons found out they were going to have a trail. Their lawyer, Henry, had passed on the message. They immediately got nervous. They wasn't sure had to even dress.

They both looked at each other and got excited. Somehow, they both were thinking the same thing. They were closer to getting their son back.

Meanwhile, Arthur's lawyer told him they was going to trail. Officer Johnson tried to get him to confess. Or at least tell them where Eric was at. Arthur just kept quiet.

The next day was the day of the trail. Henry, who was wearing a black suit, told the Thompsons to remain calm. Mary wore a red dress and heels. David wore khakis and a button-up shirt. They were both sweating as they entered the courtroom. They sat down on the upper right. The jury of seven people came in the room. They sat in the jury box. Then, Arthur, in an orange jumpsuit, came into the room. Mary or David tried not to stare. Arthur and his lawyer sat across from the Thompsons. Officer Johnson was also there. He was sitting in the back.

Then all of a sudden, the judge came into the room. Everyone stood up. When she sat, everyone sat back down. Her name was judge Hawthorne. She looked to be in her fifties with blonde short hair. She looked at Arthur. The expressions on his face was scared and confused.

"Will the defendant please stand up?" Judge Hawthorne asked. Arthur stood up. He was very nervous.

"The bail is set to $50,000. That is all." She said as she hit her gavel on the desk. She stood up as the crowd began talking. She left the room.

Arthur has gasped as the crowd mumbled. He was then escorted out of the room by his lawyer.

The Thompsons just had blank stares on their faces. They didn't know whether to be happy that the man was in jail or felt a little bad for him. Their lawyer turn towards them.

"Well, that's what you get for committing a crime." He said with a smirk.

As the room emptied, Mary and David also left. They talked to their lawyer afterwards or more like listened to him. He loved to talk. He was just reassuring them that they were going to win. Again, they didn't care about winning, they just wanted to get their son back.

Arthur went back to his jail cell. His lawyer wanted him to see a doctor. He call a physician, Dr. Bloom. He was short with black hair and a little overweight. He ran some tests on Arthur. Then he told Michael that the results would be back soon. He left the jail and so did Michael. They left Arthur alone and confused as he awaited his second trail.

A few days passed by. People would ask David or Mary about the trail. They didn't say much or anything at all. Meanwhile, Arthur would pace around his cell. Sometimes, he would get yelled at by the other inmates. All of a sudden, he remembered something.

"Hey, I remember something. I wanna talk to an officer!" Arthur exclaimed. Officer Johnson heard him and walked towards his cell.

"What is it?" Officer Johnson asked.

"The boy that you're looking for. I remember now. He's at my house." Arthur responded. Arthur looked sad and guilty.

He told officer Johnson his address and started to apologize. Officer Johnson quickly got into his car. He let it slip to the Thompsons what Arthur had told him. They wasn't suppose but David and Mary got into their car. They didn't care if they just got yelled at. They went to the police station in a flash. Luckily, they saw officer Johnson's car leave. They followed him to Arthur's house.

When they got there, they noticed the door was opened. It was a small one-story gray house. There were no vehicles parked at the house. Arthur's truck was moved to the police station wh

"What are you doing here?" Officer Johnson asked. He had walked in the room behind them.

"He's not here." David said.

All three of them walked out of the house. They got into their vehicles and drove off. The Thompsons went back to their house. Where could Eric be?

Officer Johnson went back to the jail. He questioned and yelled at Arthur. He told him they didn't find Eric. Arthur cried and pleaded.

* * *

Days ago... Eric waited for the bald man to come back. He eventually got tired and went to bed. The next morning, he tried to look for him. He was nowhere in sight. He really wanted to go outside. He didn't want to get in trouble though. Instead, he decided to eat cereal and watch TV. He played with legos and blocks. He played all day as another day passed. And another day passed after that. He got tired of waiting. He put on his shoes and went outside.

The day of the trail was here. Mary was shaking as she got dressed. She had on a gray dress with floral print all over the dress. David stood next to her. He was dressed in khaki pants and a green button up shirt.

"You look great honey." He said as he hugged her tight. He kissed her on the cheek. He also was nervous.

They said a quick prayer before they left. When they got to the courthouse, there was reporters outside the door. Their lawyer greeted them and escorted them inside the courthouse. All three came inside the courthouse and sat on the right side. Mary and David felt the pit of their stomach drop as soon as they sat down. Haddock wasn't nervous at all. He seemed confident. If he said anything, it was followed by a cocky grin.

Arthur and his lawyer finally came into the room. They sat down on the left side of the room. Judge Hawthorne came into the room and everyone stood up. She sat at the front of the room.

"Please. Be seated." She said. Everyone was seated.

The jury looked concerned. The Thompsons tried not to look at Arthur. But then again, they wanted to scream at him.

"I will let each lawyer state their case. The plaintiff's lawyer can go first." Judge Hawthorne said.

Mary and David was already staring at the judge. They were so nervous and already sweating. Haddock stood up and walked over to the jury. He smiled with another cocky grin.

"As my first witness, I would like to call Mary Thompson to the stand." Haddock requested. This wasn't a surprise.

He had already talked to the Thompsons about

calling them to the stand. He could only chose a certain amount so instead of calling David, he chose Mary. Mary stood up and walked to the front. Officer Johnson walked towards her with a Bible.

"Place your hand on the Bible please." He said. Mary nervously placed her right hand on the Bible.

"Do you swear to tell the truth and nothing but the truth?" Officer Johnson asked.

"Yes, I do." Mary said. Officer Johnson took the Bible and went back to sit down. Mary walked towards the stand. She sat down in a chair near the judge.

"Now, Ms. Thompson, can I ask you a few questions?" He asked as he faced Mary.

"Yes." She replied.

"Can you tell me what happened on the day Eric got kidnapped?" Haddock asked.

Mary had to relive that horrible day. As she did, she told the court everything. She started to tear up.

"Thank you, Ms. Thompson." Haddock said. Haddock went back to his seat.

Michael stood up and went towards Mary.

"Ms. Thompson, did you actually see my client take you boy?" Michael asked.

"No, I didn't see his face." Michael interrupted. It left Mary kind of speechless.

"That is all." Michael said. He went back to his seat.

"You may step down." Judge Hawthorne told Mary. Mary quietly stepped down and went back to her step.

"Mr. Robertson, you can call your witness?" Judge. Hawthorne said. Michael stood up.

"I would like to call officer Johnson to the stand." He said. He unbuttoned his suit he was wearing. Officer Johnson came to the stand where another officer read his rights. After that, he had a seat.

"Officer Johnson, I understand that you searched my client's house?" Michael asked.

"Yes, I did." He replied.

"And did you find young Eric at my client's house?" He asked.

"No, I didn't. He wasn't there." He replied.

"That is all. Thanks." Michael said. Officer Johnson stepped down. He went back to his seat in the back.

"Judge, I would like to call on one more witness." Michael requested.

"Go ahead." She said.

"I would like to Dr. Bloom to the stand." Michael looked backed to the doctor. He was in the crowd of people sitting on a bench.

The doctor got up and came to the stand. He then got read his rights. Afterwards, he sat down on the witness stand.

"Dr. Bloom, when my client was arrested, did you examine him?" Michael asked.

"Yes, I did." Dr. Bloom answered. Haddock stood quickly.

"Judge, we didn't know he was going to be examined by a doctor." Haddock almost yelled at the judge.

"Don't speak out of turn Mr. Haddock." She said. Haddock sat back down in his seat. He was frustrated.

Michael gave Haddock a smirk then turn to face the doctor again.

"So, Dr. Bloom, what did you find out about my client?" Michael asked.

"He has Alzheimer's. He tends to forget a lot of details." He said. People gasped at what the doctor said.

"I also did research and found out that he lost his wife and son in a car wreck. His son was Eric's age when he passed. They actually resemble each other.

Arthur looked down and felt sad. Mary and David looked at each other. They held hands tightly.

The lawyers went back and forth trying to convince the jury. Then eventually the jury went to the back to discuss their verdict. After they came out, they sat down in their seats. They had their verdict.

"Alright, Arthur, please stand. Do you have anything you would like to say before you hear your verdict?" The judge asked. Arthur stood up.

"Yes. Have mercy on me. I am a confused man. I was just seeking my son. I saw him and wanted to help." Arthur said.

"Stop! We want to drop the charges!" David shouted. The crowd got nosily. Then Mary stood up.

"As long as he gets help then we'll drop the charges." Mary said.

"Order! Order!" The judge said as she was banging her gravel on the stand. She looked at Mary.

"Are you sure? You will have to fill a report and cancel this case. Do you want to do that?" She asked Mary.

"Yes." Mary said.

"What? We was going to win!" Haddock said throwing his hands up in the air.

"Quiet. All you care about is the money." Mary said.

"Officer Johnson, please escort Arthur to the back please." Judge Hawthorne said.

Mary ran up to Arthur as Officer Johnson was trying to take him to the back. David followed behind her. Arthur was in handcuffs and Officer Johnson had him by the arm.

"Please tell me where our son is!" Mary exclaimed as she got in Arthur's face.

"I don't know. He should have been at my house."

He paused. "I am so sorry. I was confused." He responded.

"We let you off the hook so please tell us. Try to remember." David said as he was holding his wife back. He tried holding her close to him.

"He was at the house. I don't know where else he could be." Arthur said.

Arthur got escorted out of the room. Michael followed behind him. Arthur was going to get the proper care he needed.

The Thompsons just stood there. They thought, if they showed him forgiveness then they would get Eric back. Sure, Arthur would get help but what about their son? They said nothing to Haddock as he stormed out of the room. They eventually got into their vehicles and went home.

Have they lost all hope? Where was Eric? They pulled up to their driveway and got out of the vehicle.

All of a sudden, a ball came rolling towards them. Then a miracle happened, Eric came from around the house. Mary and David both gasped.

"Mom! Daddy! I found you and my ball." Eric shouted. They ran towards each other. They hugged and kissed each other. They couldn't believe it.

He's here. Eric is here. Safe.

Printed in the United States
by Baker & Taylor Publisher Services